FOOTBALL
CRAZY

FOOTBALL CRAZY

TONY BRADMAN

With illustrations by
Michael Broad

Barrington Stoke

For Oscar, my favourite footballer!

First published in 2013 in Great Britain by
Barrington Stoke Ltd
18 Walker Street, Edinburgh, EH3 7LP

www.barringtonstoke.co.uk

Reprinted 2014, 2017

Text © 2013 Tony Bradman
Illustrations © 2013 Michael Broad

ISBN: 978-1-78112-212-9

Printed in China by Leo

Contents

Chapter 1
Not Much Fun

'What a great day to play football,' Danny Lee thought as he ran out of the old shed where the teams got changed. There had been some rain earlier, but it had stopped now, and the pitch was perfect – not too damp, but not too hard either.

"Hey Danny, your ball!" his friend Jamil called out.

Danny looked up and saw the ball dropping towards him out of the sky. He took it on his chest, let it fall to his thigh, then hit it back on the volley. Jamil stuck a foot out to stop it, but the ball flew into the goal behind him.

"He shoots – he scores!" Danny laughed.

"Pretty cool," said Lewis, his other friend. The three of them had been best mates since Infant School, and they had joined Redpath Rovers together. "It's just a shame you don't do that in matches," Lewis teased. "We might win a few if you did."

"It's not just down to me, is it?" said Danny, as he collected the ball from the back of the net. "You should shoot a bit more often yourself – here you go!"

Danny tapped the ball out to Lewis, who tried a shot and totally fluffed it. Danny and Jamil fell about laughing, and they laughed a lot more over the next few minutes. They were all

football crazy. They always had a kick-about before a game, when they tried tricks with the ball and pretended they were superstars. Danny sometimes thought this was the part of being in a team he enjoyed the most.

It's a shame the real games weren't as much fun. Last season they had lost every game they played, usually by at least four or five goals. This season looked like it was going the same way. So far they had played three games, and lost 3–0, 4–0 and 6–0. Last week they hadn't even got close to scoring, and their coach Mr Perkins said they were lucky not to have let in a lot more goals from the other team.

At last Mr Perkins came out onto the pitch. "Right lads, gather round!" he shouted. Mr Perkins was well into his 60s, and the truth was that he didn't know an awful lot about football. But nobody else had wanted to coach the team. "He's mad," Danny's dad had said. "He's a retired teacher. You'd think he'd suffered enough."

Danny ran over with Lewis and Jamil to join the rest of the team. They formed a circle round Mr Perkins as they waited for his usual pre-match pep-talk. Danny looked them over. They were definitely a very mixed bunch of boys – a whole range of sizes and shapes. At least their kit wasn't too bad. The team was sponsored by Jamil's dad, who had his own small IT company.

A few die-hard parents stood round the pitch, which was one of three in their local park. None of the parents seemed too keen. The away team were also in a huddle round their coach. Both groups of boys were checking the other team out, taking crafty peeks instead of listening. Danny wasn't impressed, but you could never tell just from looking.

Mr Perkins's pep-talk was the same as ever. "Remember what we practised in training" (that would be difficult as most of them didn't go to training). "Keep your shape" (that would be a lot easier if they had any idea what it meant). And "make every ball count" (which would be fine if only they got possession of the ball from time to time).

At last the ref blew his whistle for the teams to get ready to start the game. Mr Perkins gave a deep sigh and trudged over to his usual place.

Rovers won the toss, and they chose to kick off. Danny stood next to Jamil. The ball was on the centre spot between them, and everyone was waiting.

"I don't know about you," said Jamil. "But I think we're going to win."

They lost ...

15–0.

Chapter 2
A Challenging Job

That game was on Sunday, and Danny was still brooding about it when he got to school on Monday. Lewis and Jamil went to the same school as him, and the three of them always met in the playground for a quick kick-about before they had to go in. But this morning they were waiting for him with grim looks on their faces.

"What's up with you two?" Danny asked. "Has somebody died?"

"Er … not exactly," said Lewis. "Mr Perkins has quit as our coach."

"He phoned my dad last night," Jamil said. "He said his wife is fed up with him coming home grumpy and down after every game."

"Charming!" said Danny. "What's going to happen now, then?"

Lewis and Jamil looked even more grim.

"My dad says he might not sponsor us any more since we don't have a coach," said Jamil. "It's not a great advert for his business when the team loses all the time."

"So we don't have a coach, and we don't have a sponsor …" said Danny.

"And we don't have a match on Sunday," Lewis finished for him. "It's been cancelled."

"Well, that's it, I suppose," said Danny. "Game over. No more team."

The three friends stood in silence for a moment, thinking about it.

"Well, maybe that's not such a bad thing," Jamil said at last. "I can't say I've been enjoying it much. I mean, we're always at the bottom of the league."

"It would be more fun if we won from time to time," said Lewis.

"That's not likely to happen, is it?" Jamil shook his head sadly.

"It might if we got a new coach," said Danny.

"But who would take the job?" said Lewis.

"Someone who likes a challenge?" said Danny.

Lewis and Jamil looked at each other and shook their heads as if they couldn't believe what they had heard. Then they snorted with laughter.

"Yeah, right," said Jamil. "In your dreams ..."

Danny knew it sounded daft. But to his surprise, he found he wasn't willing to leave it there. He hadn't been enjoying playing for the team either. But he didn't want to give it up. There was something cool about being in a team and playing in proper kit on a proper pitch with a proper referee.

For the rest of that day Danny couldn't stop thinking about finding a new coach. On his way home from school he made a mental list of all the grown-ups he knew – teachers, family, friends of his family, family of his friends. He was willing to consider anyone, male or female, of any age. But no one seemed right, and by the time he got home he was very fed up. He made himself a drink and raided the biscuit tin, then slumped down on the sofa in front of the TV.

"Bad day? I'm listening," said his mum. She sat next to him on the sofa with a cup of tea and pinched one of his biscuits. Danny's two younger brothers were yelling at each other upstairs, but that was nothing new.

Danny told her what had happened. "We need a new coach," he said. "That would save us. But I haven't got a clue where we can find one."

"Well, I just might be able to help you there," his mum said with a smile. "You know Liz who I work with?"

Danny didn't, but he nodded as if he did.

"Well," his mum went on, "Liz was telling me about her uncle, or was it her sister-in-law's stepfather? I can't remember ... Anyway, *somebody* Liz is related to used to be some sort of coach for a big team, but he's retired now. Do you want me to ask her about him?"

"Do I?" said Danny. He sat up. "You bet I do."

Maybe the team wasn't dead yet …

Chapter 3
Enter the Dragon

Danny made sure his mum rang Liz that same evening. After the call, Mum still wasn't sure how the man was related to Liz, but at least she had a name for him. It didn't ring any bells with Danny, but his dad seemed to know who he was.

"Jock Ramsey?" Dad said at dinner. He frowned. "Oh, yes, he was very well known at one time. I had no idea he was still alive. Very old school ..."

Danny looked Ramsey up on the web. He'd played professionally until an injury forced him to pack it in. He'd coached in the semi-pro leagues to begin with. Then he'd managed some decent second division sides. He ended up at a club that had been big once, but then had struggled for years. With Ramsey on board, they won a couple of titles in the lower divisions. Then they had a few good runs in the FA and League cups. Ramsey retired when the club went bust.

There were plenty of pictures. Danny peered at the face on the screen in front of him. The dates meant that Jock Ramsey must be about the same age as Mr Perkins, but he looked younger. He had very short hair, and a face that seemed to have been made for glaring. Danny couldn't find a single picture of him smiling. Maybe that was a good thing. A coach had to be tough, after all.

A couple more calls between Mum and Liz, and Danny had Jock Ramsey's number. He passed it on to Jamil, who passed it on to his dad. The next morning Lewis and Jamil were waiting at school for Danny with big grins on their faces.

"My dad made the call," Jamil said. He sounded excited. "Your guy didn't say much – but he *is* coming to watch us train tomorrow night."

"We'd better make sure everyone turns up," said Danny. "He won't be very impressed if there's only three or four of us like last week."

"Hey, don't worry," said Lewis. "All we have to do is ring round and tell them they have a choice. Either they come to training or they're out of the team."

Danny and Jamil looked at each other, and nodded in approval.

"I like it," said Danny. "That's the way it should be ..."

More phone calls were made that evening, and Danny got a pleasant surprise at the response. Word had got round fast about Jock Ramsey, and everyone was keen to come along and meet him. Mind you, it was one thing to say that you were coming along, and quite another to turn up on the day. But when Danny arrived at the park the next evening, he saw several dads waiting outside the old shed. And inside the shed was the whole Redpath Rovers squad.

"Blimey," Danny muttered to Lewis and Jamil. "This is a first."

"I know," said Lewis. "I thought I'd come to the wrong place."

"Shh, you two!" Jamil hissed at them. "It's him, he's arrived!"

Danny looked round and saw Jamil's dad come into the old shed with Jock Ramsey. It was odd to see the real man after looking at all those pictures of him. In the flesh, he was much shorter and broader than Danny had imagined. But he *was* glaring, and Danny thought that he looked like a dragon who was preparing to destroy its enemies with a blast of fire.

"Well, boys," Jamil's dad said. "I'm sure you're just as excited as I am that we might have a new coach. I'd like you all to say hello to Jock ..."

Jock turned his head to glare at Jamil's dad.

"That would be *Mr* Ramsey," growled the older man.

"Your dad is *toast*," Danny whispered to Jamil. But he was smiling when he said it.

Chapter 4
A Bit Scary

Jamil's dad acted as coach for the training session. He got the lads to work in groups, then play a practice game. Mr Ramsey stood on the touchline with his arms folded and watched every move. The other grown-ups watched him.

It was a strange evening. There was no laughter, no banter, and no messing about. Mr Ramsey's dragon stare made all the lads nervous. So there were even more missed passes, fluffed shots and clumsy tackles than usual. Danny felt a deep gloom spread through him like a black cloud. No way would someone like Mr Ramsey want to be the coach of such a useless team.

At the end of the evening, most of the lads trooped back into the old shed to get changed. Mr Ramsey turned on his heel and headed for his car. Jamil's dad scuttled after him. Danny looked at Lewis and Jamil, and the three of them followed.

Jamil's dad caught up with Mr Ramsey by the park gate, and the three boys ducked behind a tree so they could watch and listen.

The talk between Mr Ramsey and Jamil's dad was short and one-sided. Jamil's dad opened his mouth to speak, but Mr Ramsey spoke first.

"I'll take the job," he growled. "Extra training this week – tomorrow."

He got in his car and drove away. Jamil's dad stood there looking stunned.

Danny, Lewis and Jamil grinned at each other, and rushed off to tell the rest of the squad. The lads were pleased, of course, and no one even seemed to mind about the extra training session. But they didn't seem as happy as Danny had thought they would be. He realised that he wasn't that happy either. It was good that Mr Ramsey had taken the job – but he was a bit scary to have as coach.

It was pretty much a miracle but the whole squad turned up the next evening for training as Mr Ramsey had ordered. Several more dads turned up too. Once the lads were out on the pitch, Mr Ramsey made them all gather round him in the same way that Mr Perkins had always done. But that's where the similarity between the two coaches ended. Mr Perkins was soon totally forgotten.

Mr Ramsey stared at the boys with his dragon eyes long enough to make them feel very uncomfortable. He looked each of them up and down. Danny could see he was taking note of their scruffy training kit and dirty boots.

"If you think you're going to get some kind of big speech from me, you can forget it," Mr Ramsey growled at last. "I only have three rules for the teams I run. One – you do what I say. Two – you work hard. Three – you don't talk back. Ever. Is that clear?"

There was a lot of mumbling of "Yes, sir" and "Yes, Mr Ramsey".

"Right, let's get started then," said Mr Ramsey. "You're the most unfit bunch of players I've had the bad luck to meet in my life, so we'll start with a run. Ten laps of the pitch, and whoever comes in last does it again."

"Ten laps?" squeaked Lewis in horror. He wasn't the only one.

"It'll be twenty laps for you now, son," Mr Ramsey growled. He glared at Lewis. "That's what you get for breaking rule three. So what are the rest of you waiting for? Maybe I'll decide you should all do twenty laps ..."

Two hours later Danny sat down on a bench in the old shed and leaned back against the wall. Every part of him was sore, and he was soaked in sweat.

"Kill me now," said Lewis. "I have to end the pain."

"I can't," said Jamil. "I don't have the energy."

"Stop moaning, you two," said Danny. "This is doing us good."

At least he hoped it was ...

Chapter 5
Little Red Crosses

Mr Ramsey made them train again on Thursday evening, and on the following Saturday and Sunday mornings as well since they had no match. They trained on Tuesday and Thursday of the next week too. The whole time they worked on their fitness.

"Are we training this Saturday morning as well, Mr Ramsey?" Danny asked at the end of the Thursday session. He wasn't so sore after training now, and he was even beginning to feel quite fit. Most of the other lads were the same.

"No, son, we've got a game on Sunday," said Mr Ramsey. "So you can all have Saturday off. Make sure you're properly rested – and be here an hour before kick-off on Sunday. We'll have a lot of preparation to do."

Danny, Lewis and Jamil looked at each other and raised their eyebrows. Lewis mouthed "*An hour?*" at the other two. It did seem over the top, Danny thought. But it was clear that Mr Ramsey knew what he was doing.

When Sunday came, Danny got to the park an hour and *15 minutes* before the game, just to be on the safe side – only to discover that everyone else was there already.

There was another surprise waiting for him in the old shed. Their changing room had been cleaned and swept, and brand new shirts were hanging on the hooks above the benches.

It was like a scene from an old story, where the fairies pay a visit to a house in the night and transform it with their magic. But Danny knew this had been organised by a dragon, not by fairies.

In the corner was a flip-chart. Once the boys were changed, Mr Ramsey ordered them to sit on the benches while he told them the tactics for the match. He drew a simple plan of the pitch and marked their positions with little red crosses.

"We're going to play four at the back today, and five across the middle," he said. "And we'll have one striker upfront. That's you, Danny."

"Er … isn't that a bit … defensive, Mr Ramsey?" said Lewis. "I mean, it's going to be hard for Danny to score if he's all on his own in their area, isn't it?"

Mr Ramsey's jaw twitched as he glared at him. It was clear he was trying to decide if

Lewis had broken the third rule again. Lewis looked nervous.

"Don't you worry about that, son," Mr Ramsey growled at last. "First things first. The team's job today is to make sure it doesn't let any goals *in*, OK?"

All the boys murmured, "Yes, sir." Mr Ramsey talked for a little longer, telling them that they had to stay in their positions at all times.

So that's what *keeping your shape* means, Danny realised with a grin.

And it worked. The other team were pretty good – they were six places above Rovers in the league. But when the ref blew his whistle for half-time, the score was still nil–nil – which was a real feat, given the Rovers' record. There were quite a few dads on the touchline, and some mums too, and there was a real buzz as the lads came off for Mr Ramsey's half-time talk.

Mr Ramsey didn't smile. "Keep it up, lads," he said. "Just stay focused."

Things stayed on track in the second half. The other team did a lot of attacking, but Rovers held them off, and Danny even got in a couple of shots.

Then disaster struck. In the last seconds of the game, Lewis missed an easy tackle on the edge of the box. The opposition striker burst through and scored. The ref blew his whistle, and the lads trudged off, heads down.

Mr Ramsey just turned on his heel and walked away.

Chapter 6
Life and Death

Mr Ramsey gave Lewis a dragon-style roasting at the next training session. He also made Lewis tackle everyone else in the squad, over and over again. And every time Lewis missed a tackle, he had to do five laps of the pitch as well.

It was the toughest training session so far, and Mr Ramsey gave them all a very hard time. Danny couldn't understand it. They had played better on Sunday than ever before, and they

had only lost by one late goal. But Mr Ramsey was treating them as if they had lost on purpose and needed to be punished. By the end of the session there were a lot of tired, grumpy faces.

"That wasn't much fun," Jamil muttered as they trudged off the pitch.

"Who said football was supposed to be fun?" growled Mr Ramsey. Jamil hadn't noticed their coach was behind him. "Ever heard of Bill Shankly, son?" Ramsey asked.

"Er … no, Mr Ramsey," Jamil squeaked.

"No?" said Mr Ramsey. A look of pain and disbelief passed across his face. "What in the name of all that's holy do they teach you kids in school these days? Bill Shankly was one of the greatest football managers of all time. He once said 'football isn't a matter of life and death – it's far more important than that'. If you wanted fun, you should have joined the Guides. I'm all about *winning*."

"Now I feel really depressed," Jamil moaned as Mr Ramsey walked away.

"He didn't mean it," said Lewis. "He was joking ... wasn't he?"

"I don't think he does jokes," said Danny.

The next couple of weeks were a blur of training, more training, and deadly serious talks about tactics by Mr Ramsey. There were changes, too. Danny and his friends arrived at one training session to discover that some old faces had gone – and a lot of new ones had appeared. There were half a dozen new players, big lads who didn't take any prisoners when it came to tackles.

"How old are they?" Danny said. "They look as if they're already shaving."

"My dad told me Mr Ramsey sorted everything out with the league," Jamil said with a shrug. "Nobody is going to argue with a man like him, are they?"

There were matches, too, of course – and the most amazing thing about them was that Redpath Rovers *even started to win*. Only by the odd goal at first – a 1–0 victory thanks to a penalty, then a hard match that ended 2–1 to Rovers. The league wasn't that big – only ten teams – and Rovers leap-frogged the teams above them to reach the middle of the table.

"Have you noticed how much ... *louder* the games are these days?" Jamil asked as they came off the pitch one Sunday. "I can't hear myself think."

Jamil was right, Danny thought. Almost all the parents came to watch the games now, and lots of other people he didn't know. They got very excited and cheered and booed. Sometimes they even yelled at the referee, although they weren't supposed to. A Rovers dad had almost got into a fight with another dad who had come with the other team, but their wives had calmed them down.

It was great to be part of a winning team, of course. Sometimes Danny almost wanted to pinch himself to see if he was dreaming. Rovers winning games? Sitting pretty, half-way up the table? It just didn't seem possible. Danny had been scoring goals too, good ones – a great volley, a couple of diving headers. But he couldn't help thinking that it was all getting, well ... a little bit *serious*.

And that was even before the game with the team at the top of the league.

Chapter 7
The Big Leagues

The pressure started to build very early. In fact, the heat was on from the end of the game on Sunday. Mr Ramsey made the lads wait after they'd got changed so he could talk to them. Not about the game they'd just played – about the next one.

"OK, lads," he said. "Big game coming up, so we need to put in some extra effort this week. We'll be training every night, and on Saturday as well."

"But what about stuff like homework?" said Jamil. "We get a lot."

Mr Ramsey turned to glare at him with his dragon eyes.

"Read my lips, son," he growled. "*Homework is not important.* Right, off with you now – except you, Danny Lee. I'd like a wee word."

Danny sat frozen on the bench while the others hurried out. Lewis and Jamil grinned and pretended to slit their throats behind Mr Ramsey's back.

"I know what you two are doing," Mr Ramsey snarled at them. "Take no notice of your pals, Danny," he went on, as they shut the door behind them. "I'm not going to give you a hard time. I just wanted to ask if you'd ever thought of trying to make it as a pro."

"What, me?" Danny squeaked in surprise. "Er ... no, I haven't."

"Well, maybe you should," said Mr Ramsey. "I can't promise anything, but I reckon you might have what it takes. I've still got a few contacts in the game. I could have a word, if you like. Anyway, have a think about it, let me know ..."

Danny found it hard to think of anything else over the next few days. Lewis and Jamil were very impressed, and kept going on about it all the time.

"Will you still talk to us when you're rich and famous?" Lewis asked.

"Yeah, and will you let us have a ride in your Ferrari?" begged Jamil.

Danny gave a hollow laugh. Of course what Mr Ramsey had said was very flattering. But Danny didn't know whether he wanted to take him up on his offer. The pressure on Danny and his mates was growing with every training session. Lots of parents were coming along, and everyone was getting hyped-up about the big game on Sunday. It was all starting to make Danny nervous.

So what must it be like for grown-up professionals in the big leagues?

Sunday came round a little sooner than Danny would have liked. He felt a little sick when he arrived at the park. He could hear the buzz from the parents and other spectators on the touchline. There was already a large crowd. Danny got changed with the other lads and listened to Mr Ramsey's team talk. It was all about hitting the other team hard, and not letting them hit back.

"Sounds more like a war," Lewis muttered as they ran onto the pitch.

Five minutes into the game Danny found himself thinking that war was exactly what it was like. The other team had some big lads in defence, and they clattered into him every time

he got anywhere near the ball. There were lots of yells and boos from the crowd, and some of Danny's team got angry and complained to the ref. But the big lads in the Rovers' defence were doing just the same.

At half-time it was still 0–0. Mr Ramsey told the boys to keep giving as good as they got. He held Danny back as the lads went on for the re-start.

"This could be a tight game," he said in Danny's ear. "So if they tackle you in their area, make sure you go down as if you've just been shot by a sniper."

"What, you mean you want me to *dive*?" Danny said, shocked.

"I want you to do whatever it takes to win," said Mr Ramsey.

Danny stared at him. He couldn't believe what he'd just heard.

Chapter 8
A Red Card

Danny didn't dive in the second half. In fact, he tried even harder to stay on his feet when he was tackled in the other team's area. He just couldn't bring himself to do what Mr Ramsey had told him to. It wasn't right to cheat.

But it was clear the other team didn't mind cheating. Their tackles got harder, and Lewis was injured and had to go off. But they didn't stop there. They did lots of tugging on shirts and tripping players up when the ref wasn't looking. And when he did see what they were doing and blew his whistle, they gathered round him and argued. They yelled and shouted and told him that he'd got it all wrong.

Each set of supporters did plenty of yelling and shouting themselves every time the ref did something they didn't like. Then the other half of the crowd would start to yell and shout at them. At one point there was almost a fight, only this time it was two mums who had to be pulled apart. Even the boys on the pitch stopped to look.

"I think this is all getting a bit out of hand ..." Jamil muttered.

"They're grown-ups," said Danny. "They should be ashamed."

Danny tried to play his normal game. He managed a couple of good shots, and one even clipped the bar. But then it all went wrong. Jamil got clattered in a tackle, and Danny lost his temper. He rushed in and shoved the big defender who had hurt his friend. The ref hadn't seen the tackle, but he saw what Danny did. Out came the red card, and Danny trudged off the pitch.

There was a round of boos – one half of the crowd was angry with Danny, and the other half was angry with the ref. 'They're crazy,' Danny thought. 'Totally football crazy, and not in a good way.' He shrugged and kept walking, heading for the old shed.

"Hey, where do you think you're going?" Mr Ramsey growled at him. Danny stopped and looked at him. "You do realise you've probably cost us the game, don't you?" Mr Ramsey went on. "They're bound to score against us now."

"So it's all down to me, is it?" said Danny. "Well, that's OK. I quit."

Then he turned on his heel and walked away.

Rovers did lose, and Lewis and Jamil quit the team too. Jamil's dad pulled his sponsor money, but Mr Ramsey soon found another sponsor. The last Danny heard was that he'd changed the name of the team and found them a different pitch.

"Good luck to them," said Lewis as the three friends walked home after school one day. "I'm not going to miss being made to run extra laps."

"Me neither," said Jamil. "Mind you, it did feel good being that fit."

"I've been doing a bit of thinking," said Danny. "There are other teams and other coaches. I mean, they can't all be like Mr Ramsey, can they?"

"You're right," said Lewis. His eyes had gone wide with excitement. "Maybe we could ask round and find another team. A better team, with good players."

"And a coach who doesn't cheat," said Jamil.

"Good, that's settled, then," said Danny.

They kept walking. After a while they came to another park, one that had a couple of football pitches. The boys looked at each other and smiled. Lewis produced a ball from his bag – he never went anywhere without one.

A few minutes later they were having a kick-about on the pitch. Just the three of them. Danny realised he hadn't had so much fun in ages.

If you enjoyed *Football Crazy*, you might like these other fun books by Tony Bradman ...

Robbie wants to play for the coolest team in town, Top Grove FC. But first Top Grove want to see him play – in his own team.

The problem is, he hasn't got one!

Can Robbie get a squad into shape and onto the pitch?

www.barringtonstoke.co.uk

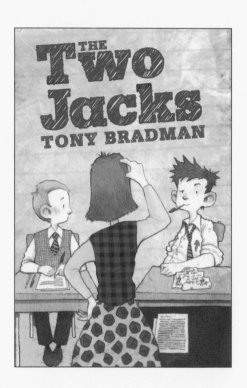

Jack Baker is the Perfect Pupil. He does his homework and never, ever does anything wrong.

Jack Barker is the Bad Boy. He gets into trouble and never, ever does anything right.

Everyone knows what the two Jacks are like. Until a new teacher gets them mixed up – and everything changes ...

Our books are tested
for children and young people by
children and young people.

Thanks to everyone who consulted on
a manuscript for their time and effort in
helping us to make our books better
for our readers.